SUPER TURBO

SAVES THE DAY!

By Lee Kirby
Illustrated by George O'Connor

SCHOLASTIC INC.

ISBN 978-1-338-35606-9

12 11 10 9 8 7 6 5 4 3 2 1   18 19 20 21 22 23

Printed in the U.S.A.   40

First Scholastic printing, October 2018

Designed by Jay Colvin
The text of this book was set in Little Simon Gazette.

CONTENTS

1

ALL QUIET IN CLASSROOM C

BEHOLD: SUNNYVIEW ELEMENTARY SCHOOL! INSIDE THESE WALLS THERE IS A BIG SECRET!

But for now it was perfectly quiet at Sunnyview Elementary. No kids running down the halls, no teachers giving out pop quizzes, no second-grade students reaching into Turbo's cage—

Oh, who's Turbo, you ask? He's this little guy here.

If you couldn't guess, Turbo is a hamster. His fur is mostly white, but he has a big brown spot on his back. He has little pink ears and buck teeth.

And this—er—palace is Turbo's home. Here in the corner of Ms. Beasley's second-grade class.

Turbo, you see, is the official pet of Sunnyview Elementary's Classroom C.

And even on a day like today, when the school was closed for snow, Turbo took his job as classroom pet very seriously.

He made sure to do all his regular classroom pet things.

TURBO!
OFFICIAL PET OF
CLASSROOM C

He drank some water. *GLUG, GLUG, GLUG.*

He ate some pellets. *MUNCH, MUNCH, MUNCH.*

And he ran on his hamster wheel. *SQUEAK, SQUEAK, SQUEAK.*

When he was finished, only a few

minutes had passed. Now what? Usually Turbo liked when the kids went out to recess and he got some peace and quiet. But today it was almost *too* quiet.

Suddenly, it wasn't quiet anymore. Turbo was sure he heard a rustling coming from the cubbies.

Straining his tiny ears, Turbo listened as hard as he could.

"There is definitely something there," Turbo said to no one in particular. "I'm the official pet of Classroom C, and so it is my duty to find out the source of this mystery sound!"

THERE MIGHT BE TROUBLE, SO I SHOULD BE PREPARED....

TURBO MADE HIS WAY ACROSS CLASSROOM C TO THE SOURCE OF THE MYSTERY NOISE. HE WAS SO SNEAKY THAT YOU MIGHT NOT BE ABLE TO SEE HIM. SO HERE'S SOME HELP.

THERE HE IS.

AND HERE.

OVER HERE.

IS THAT?

MAYBE?

Finally, Turbo got to where the noise seemed to be coming from. And then he saw a tail and it belonged to a totally terrible, awful, frightening . . .

ALLIGATOR?

ANACONDA?

DRAGON? WHAT WAS IT?!

THE MOST TERRIBLE, AWFUL, FRIGHTENING CREATURE

Turbo steadied himself and . . .

"Be careful!" yelled the owner of the tail that surely belonged to the most terrible, awful, frightening creature anyone had ever imagined. "If you grab my tail like that, it might break off!"

The strange new visitor turned

to face Turbo. Now that Turbo could get a good look at him, this stranger wasn't quite the most terrible, awful, frightening creature anyone had ever imagined. Unless the person who imagined him was incredibly afraid of small, green-spotted lizards.

"Who are you?" sputtered Turbo.

"I'm Leo," said the small, green-spotted lizard. "I'm from Classroom A. Who are *you*?"

Gasp! Another classroom pet?!

Turbo had always wondered if there were others like him out

there. Turbo stared suspiciously at Leo. Should he reveal his real name?

"What are you doing here in Classroom C?" Turbo decided to ask first.

"I'm here looking for Angelina," replied Leo. "Have you seen her?"

Turbo rubbed his chin. "I don't think so. What does she look like?"

"Well, she's all fuzzy, just like you. And she's got little pink ears, just like you. And she has buck teeth, just like you. Wait . . . are *you* Angelina?"

"Of course not! My name is Turbo," said Turbo. *Oh no!* He had accidentally revealed his real name!

"Oh, well," said Leo, "it didn't hurt to ask. All you fuzzy guys look the same to me."

Suddenly another rustling sound came from the reading nook. Turbo closed his eyes and listened while Leo pulled on a mysterious mask.

WITHOUT A WORD, TURBO AND LEO DARTED ACROSS THE CLASSROOM FLOOR. THEY WERE SUPER SNEAKY. SO HERE'S SOME HELP TO SEE THEM.

HERE.

THERE.

PRETTY SURE THIS IS LEO.

HERE? MAYBE?

THIS IS DEFINITELY TURBO. OR MAYBE A DUST BUNNY. IT'S HARD TO TELL.

The two stopped in front of the bookcase.

"Nice moves!" Leo said. "They were really . . . *super*."

"Uh, are you wearing a mask?" Turbo asked.

"No," said Leo. "Don't be silly."

Turbo wasn't being silly and he was pretty sure he had seen Leo actually run *up* some *walls*.

Then, on the bookcase, a book lurched out several inches from the shelf. A mysterious figure came into view. It was fuzzy. It had pink ears. It had buck teeth.

3

TURBO GETS A SUPER SURPRISE

"Angelina!" cried Leo as he pulled off his mask.

Ah, so this was Angelina. Turbo wondered what she was doing in Classroom C when she said, "Can you help me get this book? I'm tired of all the books in Classroom B. Too many pictures, not enough words."

Another classroom pet?! Turbo was flabbergasted. What a day today was turning out to be!

Angelina started pushing the book farther toward the edge of the shelf. Quick as lightning, Leo raced up the bookcase to help her.

Meanwhile, Turbo ran off to get a pillow to catch the book.

OKAY! PUSH!

On the count of three, Angelina and Leo gave a big shove, and the book fell right onto the pillow.

Leo skittered down the side of the bookcase, and Angelina simply jumped off the shelf onto the pillow. Now that she was up close, Turbo could see the resemblance.

Turbo shook his head. "I have to admit, I never knew there were any other classroom pets," he said, sort of embarrassed.

"Every classroom has its own pet," explained Angelina. She held out her hand to shake Turbo's.

Turbo rubbed his hand gingerly. "Wow, you're strong!"

"Of course I'm strong!" she said. "I'm a guinea pig and I have super-pig strength!"

Turbo's mouth fell open. "Super-pig strength?" he asked.

He also noticed that she had a perfect white *W* in the middle of her fur.

"But that's not my real super-power," Angelina added.

Superpower? What was going on? But before Turbo could respond, Leo jumped between them.

"Ha-ha, that's enough, Angelina," Leo said quickly. "Okay, well, we'll be getting along. Turbo, it was nice to meet you—"

Suddenly something fluttered onto the floor.

"Hey?" said Turbo. "Is that a . . . mask?"

Leo swiftly scooped up the mask and hid it behind his back.

But Angelina said, "It's too late now, Leo. He knows."

Leo turned around. Turbo wondered if he was about to run away. But when Leo turned *back* around, he was wearing the mask and a

supercool handkerchief with a giant
G on it.

Turbo's eyes practically popped
out of his head. Angelina was also
now wearing a mask and the *W*
on her belly almost seemed to be
glowing.

AND I'M NOT JUST ANGELINA . . .
I'M WONDER PIG!

Turbo looked back and forth between the two pets. "You! Guys! Are! Superheroes?!"

Leo nodded. "But this is top secret information, and you must promise to keep it that way," he told Turbo.

Without a word Turbo raced off. Leo and Angelina just looked at each other.

"I guess that was too much for him," said Angelina.

"Well, we are pretty awesome," said Leo.

Suddenly the caped figure leaped back into view.

Now it was Angelina's and Leo's turn to be surprised.

Leo rubbed his eyes. "Another superhero?! This is *great*! Angelina, leave your book here for now. Let's introduce Super Turbo to the team!"

4

MEET THE TEAM!

"Team?" asked Turbo.

Angelina smiled. "There aren't just other classroom *pets*," she said. "There are other pet *superheroes*! I'll show you the way."

The three heroes scampered over to the vent by the door of Classroom C. Angelina lifted the grate off the

vent so
that Turbo
and Leo could get
inside. They followed her down
the length of the duct until they
came to another grate.

"Hiya, Clever!" Leo said with a
wave as he stepped out.

In a cage way above them, a

green parakeet looked down. "Hey, Leo! Hey, Angelina! Who's that with you guys?"

"This is Super Turbo" said Angelina. "He's the pet protector of Classroom C!"

SUPERHEROES, HUH?

THEN THIS LOOKS LIKE A JOB FOR . . .

Clever unlocked her cage and flew down to them. The animals all followed Angelina through the vents. They came out into another room, filled with beakers, scales, and microscopes.

"This is the science lab. Warren lives here," explained Angelina.

Clever flew up to a glass case.

HEY, WARREN! WAKE UP! ITS TIME FOR PROFESSOR TURTLE TO STRIKE AGAIN!

Even with the other animals' help, it still took a very long time to get Warren down to the vents.

"I like your visor," Turbo told Warren.

"Thanks," said Warren. "The . . .

wings . . . make . . . me . . . go . . . faster."

Leo placed his hands where his hips would be if geckos indeed had hips.

OKAY, THAT'S ALMOST THE WHOLE TEAM!

5

SOMETHING SMELLS FISHY

Turbo had never been to the principal's office, but he knew from his time in Classroom C that it was a place to be avoided at all costs. Only students who were in the biggest trouble possible went to the principal's office. So what sort of terrifying pet would live there?! The vent in the principal's office was conveniently located right above a shelf. The room was dark as all the animals filed out one by one. Turbo noticed a big cage that was made of wire—like his—and wood.

Suddenly the lights flickered on.

Meanwhile, Angelina had grabbed a rope the pets kept stashed under the garbage can. Like a pro, she swung the rope and lassoed the door handle. Each animal grabbed onto the end, and together they pulled. The doorknob turned . . . and turned . . . and finally . . . *CLICK!* They pulled the door open.

"Wow!" Turbo exclaimed. He was very impressed.

The animals filed out of the principal's office and into the hallway. Suddenly there was a voice.

CLEVER! CLEVER, IS THAT YOU?

But how?

The pets all thought hard.

"I could build a teleporting machine," offered up Warren. "We could teleport Nell out of the fish tank!"

"You can do that?" asked Turbo, shocked.

"Well . . . I never have before," admitted Warren. "But I could try."

"Even if we could teleport Nell down here, she would still need water to breathe," Leo pointed out.

"I have an idea! Wonder Pig, come with me!" Turbo pulled his cape tight and scampered down the hall.

Angelina looked to the others, shrugged,

and ran off after him. The other animals stood around, unsure of what to do.

"So what did you do to end up here in the hallway, Nell?" asked Clever.

Nell flapped a fin, revealing a long, lightning bolt–shaped scar on her side. "It's a long story," she said. "A story for another time."

Just then, everyone stopped talking. A rumbling sound was coming down the hallway. Suddenly Super Turbo came into view. He was rolling along at superspeed in his hamster ball. Wonder Pig was running to catch up with him.

MAKE WAY FOR THE TURBOMOBILE!!

Clever and Frank barely leaped out of the way as Turbo raced toward them, coming to an abrupt stop as he bounced off Warren's hard shell. Dizzily, Turbo hopped out of the Turbomobile. "We can fill my Turbomobile with water, and Nell can ride along with us!"

Leo climbed down the wall he had scurried up. "I don't want to rain on your parade, Super Turbo, but there are holes in that hamster ball. The water will leak out."

"Yeah, but Boss Bunny, you have gum on your utility belt, right? We can chew it up and plug the holes," said Turbo.

Frank rubbed his whiskers. "That sounds almost crazy enough to work."

Clever turned to Nell. "Nell, what do you think?"

Nell looked around at the other fish in her tank, then back at Turbo. "I like this guy! He's nuts! Let's do it!"

Working together, the animal superheroes put Super Turbo's plan into action. The classroom pets with buck teeth—and a lot of the animals had them—chewed up the gum. Clever used her beak to stick the chewed-up gum into every hole. Warren noticed a bottle cap on the ground and calculated that it would take approximately 15.37 bottle caps of water to fill the Turbo-mobile. Leo scampered up the tank

and back down, carefully filling the
bottle cap and then dumping the
water into the Turbomobile.

Finally, the job was done. While
the superpets held the ball steady,
Nell leaped out of her tank and did
a perfect triple somersault dive into
the Turbomobile.

"Fantastic!" Leo clapped.

"Fantastic Fish! That can be your superhero name!" said Turbo excitedly.

"I like it!"said Nell as she swished her tail. "I'm not just Nell . . . I'm Fantastic Fish!"

SOMETHING *ELSE* SMELLS EVIL

They were all there. Super Turbo, Wonder Pig, the Great Gecko, the Green Winger, Professor Turtle, Boss Bunny, and Fantastic Fish. And they were ready to fight evil!

The only problem was ... what evil? The animals looked at one another, all clearly thinking the same thing.

"So . . . ," began Super Turbo.

"Um . . . ," said the Green Winger.

"Well, uh . . . ," added Boss Bunny.

"I'm hungry," said Professor Turtle.

"Great idea!" exclaimed the Great Gecko. "A snack! We're going to need fuel if we're planning to fight evil today."

The rest of the pets eagerly agreed. Then they crawled, scampered, hopped, flew, rolled, and otherwise walked through the doors of the empty Sunnyview Elementary cafeteria.

"Hold it!" Boss Bunny yelled. "I smell something rotten in here."

"Something rotten? Well, the school *is* closed because of the snow," the Great Gecko offered up. "Maybe they didn't have a chance to take out the trash."

Boss Bunny's pink nose twitched. "This isn't rotten garbage. This is a different smell."

"I don't smell anything," said Fantastic Fish. Although, to be fair, she was underwater.

"Yeah, Boss Bunny, how do you know what evil smells like?" asked Professor Turtle.

IT'S NOT THE NICE KIDS! IT'S THE KIDS WHO MISBEHAVE, THE KIDS WHO ARE TROUBLE. AND WHEN THEY SEE ME, THEY ALL WANT TO TOUCH ME!

 THEY REACH IN WITH THEIR HANDS, GRABBING, PETTING. . . .

 THE KIDS . . . ARE EVIL?

OH MY GOODNESS, NO. BUT THEY SURE ARE GRABBY.

AND I WISH THEY'D WASH THEIR HANDS BETTER AFTER THEY GO TO THE BATHROOM.

Suddenly Wonder Pig burst out laughing. "Boss Bunny, I'm pretty sure you're just hungry. We all are!"

The Great Gecko nodded. "Keep that nose to the ground," he told Boss Bunny. "I'm getting a snack!"

The other classroom pets ran off to the pantry, but Super Turbo hung back. Boss Bunny had seemed so sure there was evil afoot, but where? Who? WHAT? Turbo did one last scan of the cafeteria, then ran off to join his new pals.

By the time Super Turbo reached the other classroom pets, the pantry door was already open. The Great Gecko had scurried up the shelves, where he and the Green Winger threw snacks down to the others.

While everyone happily munched on chips, bagels, and crackers shaped oddly like Nell, Super Turbo noticed that Boss Bunny was still standing back, looking troubled. His nose was twitching more than ever. Super Turbo was starting to get the feeling that Boss Bunny was right. And that's when he saw it . . .

7

WHISKERFACE

A thin pink tail was sticking out of a hole in the wall.

It certainly has been a day for weird tails, Super Turbo thought.

Suddenly the tail disappeared. In its place a pair of beady yellow eyes stared out.

"Well, well, what do we have here?"

said a squeaky voice. A small hairy figure with big ears marched into the pantry.

Super Turbo stepped forward between this stranger and his new friends. He puffed out his chest and adjusted his goggles. "Stay back, Mr., uh . . . ," he paused, not sure what to call this creature.

"Whiskerface!" yelled the stranger.

"Mr. Whiskerface?" asked Turbo.

ARE YOU SURE YOU'RE A RAT? YOU SEEM PRETTY SMALL TO ME.

YEAH, YOU LOOK MORE LIKE A MOUSE. WHAT DO YOU THINK, GREAT GECKO?

BOY, I DON'T KNOW. ALL YOU FUZZY GUYS LOOK THE SAME TO ME.

YOU . . . SAID . . . IT.

I AM A RAT! A BIG, MEAN, NASTY RAT!

"I've been waiting for you all to arrive," Whiskerface said, sinisterly twirling his long whiskers. "You see, with all the classroom pets in one place, I can capture you and take over the school!" Whiskerface laughed a horrible, high-pitched laugh.

Before the super animals could respond, Whiskerface cried: "But wait! There's more! Because after I take over Sunnyview Elementary, I will use the school as my base . . . to take over the entire world!"

The pets blinked.

"I think you may have left out a few steps in that plan of yours," said Fantastic Fish.

"Enough distractions!" Whisker-face yelled. "The point is, I have you all where I want you. And now I will make you my prisoners!"

"Oh yeah?" said Wonder Pig, stepping forward. The *W* on her belly once again seemed to be *glow-ing.* "Well, look around. There's *one* of you and *seven* of us!"

Whiskerface gave a sly grin. "RAT PACK!" he suddenly commanded.

85

8

THE PLAN TO TAKE OVER THE WORLD

Through the hole in the wall, a stream of hairy, whiskered, big-eared creatures came pouring into the pantry. In seconds Super Turbo and the other classroom pets were surrounded. Super Turbo tightened his cape. This was it.

SO WHAT DO YOU PAMPERED PETS THINK OF MY RAT PACK? IMPRESSIVE, NO?

ARE YOU SURE YOU GUYS ARE RATS? MAYBE YOU'RE CONFUSED ABOUT WHAT RATS ARE.

I'M . . . A . . . TURTLE . . .

SHUT UP! RAT PACK! TAKE THEM!

In seconds the entire pantry was consumed in an epic battle of good versus evil. Wonder Pig got behind Fantastic Fish and launched the Turbomobile forward. It rolled on a perfect path, scattering Rat Packers like bowling pins. The Great

Gecko scampered back up on the table, where he and the Green Winger pelted the rats with grapes and ketchup packets. Boss Bunny climbed atop Professor Turtle's shell and fought off the Rat Packers with his eraser.

In the chaos Super Turbo saw an opening. He launched himself at Whiskerface and tackled the very

mouse-looking rat off of the bagel he was standing on. The two of them rolled around on the floor. Super Turbo's goggles were fogging up, and it was hard to see. When they cleared, he saw that Whiskerface had been stuffed *into* the bagel during the battle. And the evil rat was now wearing it like a tutu!

But at the same time, the tide had turned against the classroom pets. A group of Rat Packers was rolling the Turbomobile back and forth. Inside the bubble, Fantastic Fish looked like she was seasick.

Professor Turtle had retreated inside his own shell, and a couple of laughing Rat Packers were playing catch with his visor.

Boss Bunny had been tied up with the string from his own utility belt.

A swarm of Rat Packers had cornered the Green Winger and prevented her from flying.

The Great Gecko had almost escaped by running up a wall, but a Rat Packer got lucky and caught the tip of his tail.

Even Wonder Pig, with her super-pig strength, was captured and down for the count.

Super Turbo suddenly realized that he was the only classroom pet left standing. The fate of his new friends, his school, and perhaps the entire WORLD depended on him!

9

WHEN HAMSTERS FLY!

Super Turbo had to come up with a plan. And fast! He scanned the pantry. The Rat Pack was distracted trying to keep his new friends from escaping. Meanwhile, Whiskerface *was* escaping. And that's when Super Turbo saw it.

Now, you know that a hamster

cannot fly. Maybe if you put a hamster in a catapult or something, you could call that flying. But that's not very nice. But on this day, against these enemies, well . . . guess what? Super Turbo flew!

With a thud, Super Turbo landed atop the table in the pantry. How long before the Rat Pack noticed him? The answer was . . . not long. Already they were racing after him.

Suddenly a lightbulb went on over Super Turbo's head. Well, it didn't go on, but it was there. And there was a long string hanging from it.

Super Turbo took a deep breath. He adjusted his goggles. He fluffed up his cape. And then with all the hamster speed he could muster, he ran as fast as he could to the edge of the table, leaped into the air, and

caught the string that hung from the
lightbulb.

KLANGALANGALANG!

The sound was unbearably loud.
Especially if you happened to be

a tiny little rodent with giant ears. Everyone knows rats hate loud noises! The evil Rat Packers fell down, clutching their ears.

Whiskerface, who was trapped in the bagel tutu, ordered his Rat Pack to cover his ears. But because of the fire alarm, the Rat Pack couldn't hear him. Instead they started crawling back through the hole in the wall. Seeing that he was deserted, Whiskerface turned and ran as well.

As he did, Super Turbo was pretty sure he heard Whiskerface yell, "I'll get you, Super Turbo! This isn't the last you'll see of me!"

10

THE SUPERPET SUPERHERO LEAGUE!

Later on, in the reading nook in the corner of Classroom C, the new friends gathered to talk about their exciting day.

Angelina turned to Frank. "And I have to say, Frank, you definitely sniffed out that evil before any of us could. It's a good thing we have your super-smelling bunny nose to use from now on."

"Sunnyview is in good hands, thanks to us," said Warren, proudly.

All the pets smiled, content with themselves. All the pets but Leo. He frowned.

WHAT'S WRONG, LEO?

WELL, NELL, WE DID A GOOD JOB TODAY. WE SAVED THE SCHOOL!

WE MAYBE EVEN SAVED THE WHOLE WORLD!

I STILL THINK THERE WERE A FEW STEPS MISSING FROM THAT PLAN.

"Super!" shouted Clever.

"Pet!" yelled Nell.

"Superhero League!" cried Frank.

"And I propose that Classroom C, right here, be our meeting place," added Angelina.

All the animals agreed it was the perfect place for a team of superhero pets.

o   o   o

That night, Turbo returned to his comfy cage in the corner of Classroom C. He carefully folded up his Super Turbo gear and returned it to his secret hiding spot. He looked at

his hamster wheel, his hamster pellets, his water bottle.

Tomorrow, school would be back in session. For all the students, all the teachers, and even Principal Brickford, it would be no different from any other day. But it *would* be different. Because tomorrow, and forever after, Sunnyview Elementary was under the protection of . . .